Kid P9-DBJ-876
Choose Your Own Adventure®!

"Adventurous, funny, sometimes terrifying; you haven't lived until you've read this book, so if you want to live, read it."

Ciera Fiaschetti, age 10

"If you don't read this book, you will, and I quote, 'get payback.'"

Amy Cook, age 10

"Warning: 99% chance of death. This book might make you cry."

Cody Curran, age 11

"Step in this book if you dare, but you better beware of what's inside here."

Gabe Frankel, age 10

CHOOSE YOUR OWN ADVENTURE®

To Ramsey and Anson

And to Shannon

BEWARE and WARNING!

This book is different from other books.

You and YOU ALONE are in charge of what happens in this story.

There are dangers, choices, adventures, and consequences. YOU must use all of your numerous talents and much of your enormous intelligence. The wrong decision could end in disaster—even death. But don't despair. At any time, YOU can go back and make another choice, alter the path of your story, and change its result.

The phone rings: a scared voice on the other end is begging you for help. You trace the call to the site of an old prison that burned to the ground more than 100 years ago, taking the lives of 112 prisoners. Even though you're an expert detective, you sense that this case will be unusually creepy and dangerous. Should you answer this cry for help? The House of Danger holds many mysteries; you will encounter hostile chimpanzees, space aliens, ghosts from the Civil War, or even travel through time. This will be one case you'll never forget—if you make it out alive!

It is a Tuesday afternoon in late June. You are on your way down to your lab in your parents' basement when the phone rings. You dash into the lab and pick it up.

"I need, I need..." says a weak voice. You hear a loud click, and the phone goes dead.

Drat! You weren't ready for that. You, the aspiring detective and psychic investigator, caught off guard. You slump down into your chair. That voice really sounded desperate.

You boot up your computer and look around. The heat of the day has not penetrated your combination office and research laboratory, where you sit surrounded by the tools of your trade: infrared-activated floodlights, high-speed movie cameras, and night scopes among them. Two large bookcases stretch from floor to ceiling, crammed with titles that would drive the timid from the room: *Murder in Fun, Ghosts and Ghouls*, and *Corpses I Have Known,* to name a few.

Turn to the next page.

2

The phone rings again, and this time you are ready. You pick up the receiver before the first ring dies out. At the same time, you activate the phone tracker and voice recorder programs running on your laptop and note the time: 2:42.

"Hello," you say.

"Help, I need your hel-l-l-lp…"

Turn to page 6.

You have to admit that you are scared, but the man on the ground needs help. The only weapon you can think of is the penknife that you always carry in your pocket. You take out the knife and brandish it wildly as you run forward. The chimpanzees seem to back off, but they are still snarling. Just as you reach the man on the ground, they lope off into the bizarre ruin near the house. They swing through the ragged network of twisted beams for a few seconds and then vanish.

You turn your attention back to the man on the ground. His breath comes in short gasps that sound almost like sobs.

Turn to page 10.

4

The Marsden residence turns out to be a large, modern house located in a fashionable suburb about a half-hour's drive from your house. You see it first through a tall iron fence running along the road. The house is set back behind a broad and well-tended lawn. You park your car down the road and walk back to the gatehouse that gives access to the estate. The gatehouse is strangely old-fashioned and ornate in contrast to the main house. The heavy iron gates, inside their framework of stone, stand slightly ajar, leaving just enough room for you to squeeze through if you want to. A bronze plaque is set into the stone on the outside of one of the walls. It reads:

SITE OF HEDGE BROOK PRISON
WHICH WAS BURNED TO THE GROUND
DURING THE PRISON RIOT OF 1887.
ONE HUNDRED AND TWELVE PRISONERS
DIED IN THE FIRE.
NOTHWIN HISTORICAL SOCIETY

You glance again at the house. The front of it is constructed largely of glass. A short distance to one side of the house is what looks like a large, strange metal sculpture rising out of a number of huge blackened hunks of shattered concrete. A shudder goes through you as you realize that these forms of twisted metal might actually be the remnants of the old burned-out prison.

Suddenly a man dashes out of the house.

Turn to page 9.

"Who are you?" you ask. "What is your name?"

"I'm scared," the voice says. "They're after me."

"Get hold of yourself," you say. "I can help if you give me your name and address."

"They've got me, they've got me…"

Click. The phone goes dead again. This time, however, you were prepared. In the few seconds that you have been talking, your telephone-tracing device, which operates in milliseconds, has already found the number of the other phone as well as the name and address of its owner:

555-7259
HENRY MARSDEN
1100 HEDGE BROOK

Go on to the next page.

You copy this information down in your smartphone. Something about this call is nagging at the back of your mind. Is it that this call reminds you of your "Spider Ghost" case? It, too, started with a mysterious phone call. Even though you were quite young, you solved that case single-handedly. The citation you received from the FBI now hangs, neatly framed, on your office wall. And the generous reward you received from the Ridgeway family when you saved them from certain death has financed your specialized detection equipment.

One thing you learned from that case is that working by yourself can be a risky business. Ricardo and Lisa, two of your friends in the neighborhood, have wanted to help you on a case. Well, this is their chance. When you call their cell phones, however, they are not picking up. You leave a message for them to call you back as soon as possible.

You're eager to begin work on the case as soon as possible, but you know it might be dangerous to start off alone. Maybe you can do some Internet searching before heading out on the case.

If you decide you should go immediately to the address obtained by the phone-tracing machine, turn to page 4.

If you decide to give Ricardo and Lisa a chance to call back, turn to page 13.

"Help! Help! They're after me," the man cries. Halfway to the gate, he drops to the ground as if he had been hit by an invisible hammer. You dash through the gate and run toward the fallen figure. But something stops you in your tracks. Three snarling animals materialize in front of the house.

What are they? you wonder. Can they be huge chimpanzees? They look mean and angry. For a moment, you are frozen to the spot.

The man on the lawn can't move and needs your help. But what good to him will you be if you're mauled by the angry chimps?

If you decide that the chimpanzees are not as dangerous as they look and rush to give aid to the man, turn to page 3.

If you make a hasty retreat to your car, turn to page 29.

10

You bend down and take the paper from his fingers, and examine it for a message. It is blank on both sides. Just then the man gives one terrible gasp and lies still. Your knees are weak. This man has been frightened to death!

The chimpanzees reappear in front of the house. One of them holds a long bamboo blowpipe. He puts it to his lips and blows. You feel a breeze on your cheek. Could it be from a dart whizzing by your face?

You race back across the lawn, through the gate, and back to your car.

This feels like real danger, and you'd promised your parents you'd call the police if your safety was ever at risk, but if you wait, whoever or whatever is going on inside that house might have time to escape.

If you decide to come back later and sneak up on the house from a different direction, turn to page 14.

If you decide to call the police and report a possible murder, turn to page 63.

Things begin to add up in your mind. This place is creepy enough, built next to the ruins of the old prison. Add to this the snarling images of chimpanzees to scare off anyone getting too close to the house. It's a perfect base of operations for a gang of counterfeiters. The unfortunate man who died must have somehow stumbled into their hideout.

You ease out of your observation post in the bushes and run back to the car. You drive to the nearest telephone to inform the police. Then you check your watch: 7:23 PM. Case solved in four hours and forty-one minutes. Not bad!

Turn to page 16.

12

Several thoughts spin across your mind. Was that man Henry Marsden? Was it his house? Was he a counterfeiter? Or was he trying to escape from counterfeiters? Trying to escape seems more likely. And what about those chimpanzees? Could there be a counterfeiting animal trainer? No. That makes about as much sense as a yodeling astronaut.

You drive home to see if Ricardo and Lisa have called. You check your cell phone. Nothing yet. You put some equipment into your shoulder bag: a pair of high-powered binoculars, a small tear-gas gun, and a high-speed camera with a zoom lens.

Then back to the Marsden place. You plant yourself in a clump of bushes across the street. From here you can see the house, but no one can see you.

You scan the lawn with your binoculars. The body of the man has disappeared. All seems quiet.

Turn to page 24.

Henry Marsden...Henry Marsden...You plug the name into every search engine you can think of. As you type it over and over, you start to feel like you've heard it or read it somewhere, but you can't quite place it.

You are an avid history buff, though you are not as strong on names and dates as you are on what actually happened. You sit back in your chair with your eyes closed, your knuckles against your forehead, in intense concentration.

The thought that it's something to do with the Civil War crosses your mind. Well, it's worth a try. There might be something in the *History of Nothwin County*. Now where did you put that book? It's somewhere in your basic research library. Finally you find it: a thick, green volume, sandwiched between *Gray's Anatomy* and *Blackwell's Poison Plants and Herbs*. The book was published by the Nothwin Historical Society some twenty years ago, though you just bought it the week before for twenty-five cents at a neighborhood lawn sale. You pull the book from the shelf and run your finger down the index of famous names in the county. There it is!

Turn to page 26.

14

You drive about a mile away from the house and park the car on the side of a tree-shaded road. You check the time on your watch that doubles as a two-way radio. It is 4:35 PM. It has been almost two hours since you got that phone call.

You take out the piece of paper that you took from the hand of the dying man. You realize that it is the corner of a larger sheet of paper. Two of the edges are cut straight, and the third side is ragged where it was torn off. You hold it up to the light, almost expecting a message to be somehow hidden inside the paper itself. You start to stick the paper back into your pocket when something makes you hold the paper back up to the light again. You hadn't noticed it before, but the paper has tiny flecks of red and blue in it. Now that rings a bell— of course! The special paper that U.S. currency is printed on has those flecks in it.

Turn to page 12.

Thirty minutes later, the three of you arrive at the site where the old prison once stood. You find that this location is now occupied by a large, very modern house built—on the outside—almost entirely of reflecting glass. The front gate, by contrast, seems to be left over from the last century. A path leads from the gate across a wide lawn to the house. You drive by slowly and then park down the road. Walking back, you cross the lawn and double-check the number on the door. 1100 Hedge Brook. This is it, all right.

"Who wants to knock?" you ask. There is no answer from Ricardo or Lisa.

"I'll do it," you say. You give a firm, loud knock. The only response is a hollow echo.

"Are you sure the telephone call came from this place?" asks Lisa.

"Of course I'm sure," you reply. "I know that…"

The heavy front door of the house starts to swing slowly open.

Turn to page 19.

16

The next day the lead story in the *Nothwin Times* is:

On a tip from a well-known local detective, whose suspicions were aroused by strange occurrences around the Hedge Brook Prison ruins, police raided a nearby house yesterday, exposing a counterfeiting operation. Seized were a number of bogus printing plates and a large quantity of counterfeit money. Three men were arrested and charged with homicide as well as counterfeiting after the body of another, as yet unidentified, man was found in the basement of the house.

The End

18

You have no choice but to do as he says. You turn right at the corner. Then, as directed by the voice, you drive another two hundred feet and turn again, this time onto an unfamiliar dirt road that leads into a heavily wooded area.

"Stop here," the voice orders. There is now a beeping sound in the back seat. You realize that the gun is away from your neck. The figure in the back seat is apparently fiddling with some sort of electronic device. While his attention is away from you for a few moments, you slip your hand quickly and silently up under the dashboard of the car.

Your knockout-gas gun, disguised as a pen, is still there.

If you decide that now is the time to use your knockout-gas gun, turn to page 32.

If you decide that this is too dangerous to try right now, turn to page 34.

"Hello?" you call. No answer.

You peer inside.

"Mr. Marsden? Hello?" you call again into the gloom of the house.

When your eyes adjust to the dim light inside, you see that the house is ornately furnished. Rich red, blue, and yellow carpets cover the floors. Chinese screens, flanked by tall bamboo plants, are placed against the walls of the entrance hallway. What appear to be ancient temple carvings fill the walls and alcoves adjoining the hallway. The place looks more like a museum than a house.

As you watch, a small concealed door opens in the side of the hallway. It had been completely hidden by the intricate patterns of inlaid wood. Out of the door comes a tall, slender woman with high cheekbones and narrow eyes. Her skin is the color of ivory. She is dressed in a long, black, old-fashioned dress.

"Won't you three come in?" she says in a high, unaccented voice.

Turn to page 28.

The three of you enter the house. As you do, the door behind you closes and locks with an ominous click. You sense that there is definitely something evil—or at least alarming—going on here.

The woman leads you down a long, dark hallway to a solarium. The afternoon sunlight streams in through a high glass ceiling. White, yellow, and purple orchids are arranged in neat rows along one side of the room. On the other side of the room is a collection of plants that you don't immediately recognize.

"I see you are admiring my babies," the woman says. "These are my Venus flytraps over here. Are they not beautiful? We are all so happy here." She picks up a trowel and tenderly starts to transplant one of them. A faint buzzing comes from somewhere in the room.

"Ah, I see we have yet another visitor," says the woman. Her face lights up with a kind of ecstasy. "Come… come to my plants, little fly."

Turn to the next page.

You begin to notice a sweet smell—almost sickeningly sweet—that you hadn't noticed before. It is coming from the plants. The fly circles around and lands on one. Suddenly the fringed leaves snap shut and trap the fly inside.

The light of the room grows dim, as if a dark cloud has suddenly drifted between you and the sun. The glass walls of the house...the sweet smell.... Suddenly, you understand that you have walked into a giant Venus flytrap yourself.

Something is happening to the woman. Her image is beginning to fade. You realize that you can see right through her. Her form then begins to grow and resolidify. It transforms itself into the image of a large, angry-looking man dressed in a Civil War uniform. He has a heavy whip in his hand. You look around you. The walls have turned to a rough, darkened stone—and high above you, the skylight has been replaced by heavy bars.

Go on to the next page.

"Now I'll deal with you rebels," growls the man. "You think you can challenge the authority of Henry Marsden." As he says this, he lashes out with the whip. Sharp pain bites into your shoulder. You feel faint. As you lose consciousness and fall to the damp stone floor, you hear only the terrified screams of Ricardo and Lisa.

The End

24

Just then a long black limousine drives up to the gatehouse. Two tough-looking men get out and walk toward the house. When they are almost there, the chimps appear. The men just ignore them and go into the house. Then the chimps vanish again— into thin air.

That's it! The chimps are not real. They must be filmed and projected holograms—three-dimensional pictures made with laser light programmed to turn on and off whenever someone approaches the house.

Minutes later, the two men leave, carrying several small packages.

Turn to page 11.

26

MARSDEN, HENRY, page 93

Your heart beats a bit faster as you flip to the right page. The book gives a short biography:

Henry Marsden, born 1839, died 1887. Served in the Union Army during the Civil War. Severely wounded at the Battle of Shiloh in 1862. Appointed warden of Hedge Brook County Prison in 1880. This prison was notorious in its day for its wretched conditions and the harsh treatment of its prisoners. Contemporary accounts say that it is likely that Henry Marsden was killed in the fire that accompanied the prison riot of 1887. His remains were never recovered. Local legend states that he was murdered by the rioting inmates of the prison, and that his ghost haunts the ruins of the prison to this day.

Go on to the next page.

You are so engrossed in reading this account that a rap on the window makes you jump. It is Ricardo and Lisa. You let them in and give them a quick rundown of the case so far. They both read the account in the history book and your notes and listen to your tape of the phone call.

"This is really strange," says Ricardo.

"How's that?" asks Lisa.

"The name of the warden and this guy who called are the same."

"Anyone can see that," says Lisa.

"Okay, now want to guess where that prison was?" asks Ricardo. "I know because my dad and I were driving by there one day and he pointed it out to me."

"You're on," says Lisa.

"Out on Hedge Brook Road on the North Side."

"That means," says Lisa, "that...that..."

"Right," you say, "that either Henry Marsden is still alive or we've got a ghost on our hands. Whichever one it is, we're onto one heck of a mystery. What should we do next?"

If you decide to go to the site of the old prison, turn to page 15.

If you decide to go to the police with your story, turn to page 87.

"We're here to see Mr. Marsden," you say.

"Why, of course you are," she says.

"Is he all right?" you ask. "Earlier he called me on the phone and said he needed help."

The woman does not answer. She only beckons with her finger for all of you to follow her.

If you accept her invitation to go in, turn to page 21.

If you sense a trap, and find a reason for leaving, turn to page 41.

You decide that it is better to get back to your car—fast! You always drive with a first aid kit and some basic defensive equipment, such as your "pen" that holds two cubic centimeters of a powerful knockout-gas.

You have the ignition key out of your pocket even before you reach the car. As you quickly open the door on the driver's side and jump in, you realize that something is wrong. You are about to jump out when you feel it—a cold metal circle, like the end of a gun barrel, pressed to the back of your neck. A raspy voice commands, "Just do what I tell you or you'll be looking for a new head. Now get this car moving and follow directions. Drive down to the corner and turn right."

Turn to page 18.

You don't need the professor to tell you how to use your new powers. The energizing process has awakened in your brain all the information you need. The chimpanzees have similar powers, but since you have started out at a much higher level, your powers are much stronger than theirs.

You can telepathically "hear" and "feel" the anger of the chimpanzees as they break open the door to the laboratory. But when they charge in, they are immediately frozen by your projected force field.

"Wow! Did I do that?" you ask.

"That is only the beginning of your new powers," says the professor.

Your new mind immediately probes out through the underground complex.

"This way, professor," you say. "I know the way out."

Turn to page 40.

32

In a split second, you turn in your seat and fire the gun at the figure in the back. As you fire, you see the "man" in the back seat for the first time. You hardly know who has the more startled expression—you or the talking chimpanzee—as he loses consciousness. You back up the car and drive directly to the police station.

"I have an unconscious chimpanzee in the back seat of my car," you explain to the officer at the desk.

"Then I suggest that you drive straight to the zoo," replies the officer.

"But this is a talking chimpanzee," you protest, "and he tried to kidnap me with a gun."

The officer and his assistant look at each other as if to say, "We've got a live one here." However, they come out to the car with you.

"This is a chimpanzee, all right," says the officer. "Certainly is a big one. Not doing much talking at the moment, though."

You search around in the back seat next to the unconscious chimpanzee. You find a small control box of some sort, but you can't find a gun. What you do find is a flat metal ring. That is how he did it! After all, that's all you really felt against your neck.

Turn to page 59.

A door to your right flies open, throwing a brilliant shaft of light into the corridor. Suddenly you are surrounded by a circle of snarling chimpanzees.

They begin to close in.

The End

You slip the pen into your shirt pocket. Maybe it will help you escape later.

You come to what looks like a giant crater in the ground. A wide ramp leads down into it. The figure in the back seat orders you to drive down. At the bottom is an entrance large enough for a car. You enter and drive through a short tunnel into a large underground garage.

A number of trucklike vehicles are parked against a loading platform on one side of the garage. They look more like huge eggs with doors in the sides, and you can't see any wheels underneath. A dozen or so strange creatures—wow!—the chimpanzees again—are loading the "eggs" with large boxes.

"All right, now, out," commands the voice behind you, "and keep your hands above your head." You see your captor for the first time. No wonder his voice sounded odd. He is one of the chimpanzees.

You are led to a door on the far side of the garage. The chimpanzee inserts a plastic card in a slot. There is a slight electronic whine as the door slides back on silent hinges. Before you is a long corridor. It is lit by what look like fluorescent bulbs—but the light from them makes your skin look purple. The corridor ends abruptly at a metal door. Again the chimpanzee uses the plastic card. The door opens. The chimpanzee pushes you roughly inside, but stays outside while the door closes.

Turn to the next page.

36

It is pitch-dark inside the room. You are alone in some kind of cell. Wait! You can hear the sound of breathing. You feel around in the dark. Your hand touches something warm. Whatever it is wakes up with a cry.

"Don't touch me... don't touch—me..." a man's voice says in an anguished tone. The voice sounds very much like the one you heard on the phone.

"Aren't you the man who called earlier today?" you ask.

"Why, yes, I did make a call. The chimpanzees took my assistant, Jethro, and me to another part of this underground complex for questioning. On the way back to this cell, Jethro and I managed to break away. I think Jethro escaped to the outside, but I haven't seen him since. I have a feeling something has happened to him.

"I locked myself in a room with a telephone. I was so desperate that I dialed a number at random. I had only a few seconds before the chimpanzees were going to break in."

"But you called twice," you say.

"That's right. I got a second chance. While they were breaking down the door to one room, I fled to an adjoining room that also had a telephone. I remembered the number that I had dialed the first time and tried it again."

"What's the story with these talking chimps?" you ask.

Turn to page 70.

The energizing chamber is a large glass cylinder with a door in the side, just large enough for a person to get inside. "I'm going to activate the alpha force now," the professor shouts from the control board outside the room. "Do you feel that?"

You do. "It's like every cell in my body is jumping up and down!" you shout. "Woo-hoo!"

"Your hair is standing on end," he observes. "In a few minutes you'll have mental and psychic powers that will let you see miles into the distance, through mountains and walls. You'll be able to lift objects with your thoughts, and also read minds."

The chimpanzees are battering at the door, trying to get in.

If you try to use your new mental and psychic powers right away, turn to page 31.

If you decide to retreat back through the tunnel and have the professor explain how to use the powers on the way, turn to page 50.

38

You release the suspended box and refreeze the chimpanzees. The howling behind you stops as suddenly as if a radio had been turned off. The box comes crashing down on the concrete floor of the garage. It breaks open, sending a cascade of money into the air.

You don't have to examine the money to know that it is counterfeit. Your heightened senses tell you that. You mind-scan the underground complex again.

Go on to the next page.

This time you find the engraving equipment, the printing presses, and the trimming machines—everything needed to produce counterfeit money. And you see huge stacks of counterfeit bills. There's currency from virtually every country in the world.

"The chimps developed these egg-shaped flying machines you see in the garage," says the professor. "They planned to use them to fly all over the world, dropping money from the sky on many countries and destabilizing all of the world's economies—the ultimate 'gorilla' warfare. After this, they had planned to become the controlling power in the world."

The struggle to escape your force field has destroyed all the chimps' special powers. Now they're nothing more than just ordinary chimpanzees.

But you will keep your heightened powers for some time.

The End

40

You and the professor run down a long, curving passageway that leads back to the underground garage. As you emerge from the passageway, the chimpanzee remaining in the garage hurls one of the heavy boxes at you. Your mind-force catches it and stops it in midair. Unfortunately, in order to concentrate on the box, your mind releases the chimpanzees back in the laboratory.

They run howling into the other end of the passageway after you.

"I'll have to work on this mind-power!" you say.

Turn to page 38.

"I think we'll visit some other time," you say to the woman. "We just stopped by to make sure everything is all right."

The three of you back away from the door and start toward the car.

"Have Mr. Marsden phone me again when he has a chance," you call back.

"You think you can just come and leave that easily?" the woman shouts in a high, almost screeching voice. "You'll be sorry! You'll be sorry!"

She goes back into the house. The front door bangs shut, but her voice still seems to echo down the road. Finally it trails off. A strangely chilling breeze blows by in the hot afternoon. You all feel a tingling sensation in your bones.

You run to where you left the car. It's gone!

"I'm sure we left the car right here," you say.

"I'm really confused," says Lisa. "I definitely remember a new house just across the road from here."

"Let's go back," says Ricardo. "Maybe we've just come too far. That lady in the house scared us. I think we got mixed up."

You walk back up the road looking for the car. But now the house is gone! Where it stood just minutes ago, the old prison stands now.

Turn to page 46.

You decide that you should get to know the professor a little better before you trust him with your brain.

"Okay, so you don't want superhuman powers," he says. "Do you have any better ideas for getting us out of here?"

"Is there any way out of the laboratory besides the main door over there?"

"Come to think of it, there's a side door over here that isn't used much. It leads to a narrow corridor that goes directly to the garage."

"Let's get out of here, then," you say. "Follow me."

You and the professor run down the corridor toward the garage when suddenly several doors opening off the corridor open, and a small army of chimpanzees swarm out of them, all carrying laser guns. You are surrounded.

"Wait, stop!" you shout, but the chimps fire. You and the professor are instantly vaporized.

The End

From a safe distance, the three of you watch the soldiers break open the front gate of the prison and the firefighters spray water on the flames. Badly burned prisoners are carried out and taken away to the hospital in horse-drawn wagons, which pass you on the road. The sun is setting.

You find your way into town, which, in the present year of 1887, is two miles away. You were born in the late twentieth century, but you will finish out your life almost a hundred years earlier. You will have the distinction of being your own great-great-grandfather with knowledge that no one else possesses.

The End

46

"That lady in the house cast some kind of spell on us. We're dreaming all this," says Ricardo.

"Here, pinch me," says Lisa to Ricardo. "Ow! I didn't mean that hard. Doesn't that prove we're not dreaming?"

"Guys," you say. "This is serious. I think we've traveled back in time."

"How are we going to get home?" Ricardo asks.

Before you can say you don't know, you hear shots and cries from the direction of the prison.

"There's something going on inside there," you say. "It must be a riot—maybe the one mentioned in the history book!"

The three of you race toward the prison. You can see smoke and flames coming out of the barred upper windows. You run up to the front entrance— two large, heavy iron doors with a foot or so of space between the top of the doors and the stone lintel above. This narrow gap glows red from the flames inside.

"Open up!" you scream. "Let the prisoners out. They'll be killed!" You try banging on the doors, but they're already too hot to touch.

Turn to page 52.

As soon as the soldiers arrive, all three of you run to ask if you can help. An officer dismounts and comes toward you.

"As soon as we get those gates open, we'll need all the help we can get," he says.

The soldiers throw a long rope with a grappling hook over the top of the iron doors. They quickly hitch together a team of six horses and tie the rope to their harness. The horses tug away at the rope for several minutes.

Nothing happens. Then, with a screeching sound, the doors burst open. A tremendous ball of flame roars out of the front gate of the prison, scattering the nearby soldiers and horses. The flame subsides and turns into a huge column of smoke rising into the sky.

Turn to page 49.

The firefighters are ready with their steam-driven water pump, spraying water into the open mouth of the front gate. Soon the fire has died down enough for you and the soldiers to start carrying out the more badly burned prisoners on stretchers.

Someone shouts, "The prisoners in the dungeons are all right. Just the upper part of the prison is burning."

"Where's Marsden?" you ask.

"He has joined his brother the devil in the flames," someone replies.

The three of you work with all your energy for the next few hours, doing your best to help the burned and wounded prisoners. You are exhausted. It's late afternoon now, but the day is still terribly hot. You have to take a few minutes to rest. You sit against a tree and close your eyes for a moment. It feels so good to relax.

When you open your eyes, the prison is gone. The modern glass house is back in its place. The three of you are sitting against a tree on the side of the road.

"That was quite a dream," says Ricardo, pulling himself groggily to his feet.

"If that was just a dream," says Lisa, "what is this Civil War soldier's hat doing over there on the side of the road? And why did we all have the same dream?"

"Dream or not," you say, "at least we're back in our own time. I won't forget this day for a long time!"

The End

50

You and the professor decide you'd better retreat.

Just as the chimpanzees break into the laboratory, you both disappear into the tunnel in the wall.

"The last thing I did in there," says the professor, "was to put the controls for the energizer on self-destruct. Just a few seconds from now…"

BLAM!

The explosion rocks the room.

Fortunately, you and the professor were back in the cell before the explosion.

"That takes care of the chimps in the lab," says the professor, "but there are still plenty around. I'm afraid that they'll all decide to concentrate together to make a strong mental force field. I think I can feel it already."

"I can, too," you say. "Is it pressing inward?"

"Yes," says the professor. "They will slowly squeeze it—until we are crushed to death inside."

"What can we do?" you ask the professor.

Go on to the next page.

"Now is the time to learn how to use your new powers—and quickly. First, imagine a disc spinning in your brain. I know that sounds a bit vague, but try it and you'll see."

"I can see it," you say, "a brilliant white disc. It's almost blinding, even though I know it's not real."

"That's good," says the professor. "You are starting off well. The disc acts like an electrical generator, but it generates mental energy instead of electrical energy. Now let the energy build up. Okay, now, aim it at the force field the chimps are creating around us. Steady now. Ease in the power. Careful! Concentrate even more."

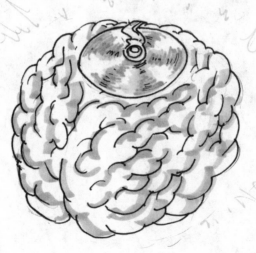

Turn to page 54.

Up on the highest rampart of the prison, you see a figure. Somehow you know it is Henry Marsden. Flames lick up into the sky around him. Even at this distance you can hear him scream.

"Help, I need hel-l-l-l-lp...."

It's the same voice you heard on the phone!

Then black smoke obscures the whole front of the prison.

In the distance, down the road, you see a troop of mounted soldiers galloping toward you. Behind them is a team of horses pulling an old-fashioned fire engine.

If you run and hide behind a tree to watch the action from a safe distance, turn to page 44.

If you stay on the road to help the soldiers, turn to page 47.

54

There is a grinding sound, followed by a deep rumble that makes the entire structure around you tremble. Then you hear a tremendous pop like the one you hear when the filament in a light bulb breaks, but much louder.

"That's it! You did it. The field is broken."

"The force field is gone?" you ask. "But I can still feel a strong energy source from somewhere in the house."

"The only way to look for whatever's producing that energy is to use your new energy to search the house, penetrating the walls with your thoughts," the professor explains. "But it will take an awful lot of energy. It might be better to get out now while we can."

If you go on a mind-search of the house, turn to page 60.

If you decide that now is the time to try to escape, turn to page 69.

"The chimpanzees sent their mind-power across the galaxy and found our planet," says the alien. "They invited an emissary from our planet to visit Earth. I was selected to go. Once I arrived on Earth, the chimpanzees imprisoned me. They refused to release me until I revealed all the secrets of my planet's technology, such as how to construct flying machines. I am very grateful to you for freeing me. I must invite you to return with me to my planet— as a hero and a welcome guest."

If you decide to accept, go on to page 57.

If you decline respectfully, turn to page 62.

"I will go to your planet," you say, "as long as my friend, the professor, can go, too."

"Very well," the alien emissary says. Suddenly you see the professor standing next to you. The strangest thing—your body is with him, though your mind is still across the room. Within seconds, you've joined it again.

"Imagine," says the professor as the two of you take your first steps into the alien ship. "Just imagine that we are the first..." Before he can finish, everything goes blank.

When you come to, you and the professor are in the midst of a crystalline city where light has never looked so beautiful, and air has never smelled so clean.

You spend several years there, learning the secrets of their advanced technology, before you return to planet Earth.

The End

58

The crashing stones so startle the single guard that you have no trouble giving him a shot of knockout-gas full in the face. The guard drops to the floor with a thud. You run across the room and slam the door. Fortunately, it locks from the inside. Just to make sure it stays shut, you push a heavy piece of lab equipment in front of it.

"Now!" cries the professor. "Get into the chamber over there. No time to waste!"

"Are you sure it's safe?" you ask.

"I would go in myself," says the professor. "But my heart can't take the shock. I'm afraid even for someone as young as you there's a risk of cardiac arrest, and permanent damage to your brain function."

If you decide to go into the super-energizing chamber, turn to page 37.

If you feel that the chamber is too dangerous and try to escape another way, turn to page 43.

The chimpanzee is still unconscious when the zoo workers come and take him off in a big cage.

As soon as you tell the officer about the man on the lawn, he and his partner take you back to the house in a patrol car. "He was right there," you insist, pointing at the blank green space. "But now he's gone."

"We can search the woods," the officer suggests, but you're too late. The body is nowhere to be found.

"The house is empty as well," the officer's partner says, emerging from the front door. "Though there's definitely evidence some kind of animal has recently been inside. And the phone's working, which is weird—the phone company has no record of anyone living here."

The following week, you go out to the zoo to have another look at the chimpanzee. You can tell that he recognizes you from the angry expression on his face when he sees you. Somehow you feel sorry for him, since you know that he can talk and now has no one to talk to—that is, unless he wants to give himself away.

You wonder where the rest of the chimpanzees have gone. No doubt they have a new hideout somewhere. You also wonder if they have claimed any new victims, like that poor man on the lawn.

The End

60

"For a mind-search," says the professor, "just project your consciousness itself, the same way you projected your concentrated energy against the force field. Have your mind leave your body. It will return if your body is threatened."

You leave your body in the care of the professor and begin to travel on mind-energy through the house. He's right—it is just a matter of complete concentration.

You trace the source of the strong energy to the center of the prison structure. There, you find a large lead-covered vault. Your mind cannot penetrate it. Instead you throw a force field around it.

A wave of anguish comes from the vault. The vault almost seems to be pleading for mercy. You release your force field. As you do, you feel a surge of even greater energy inside of you.

Suddenly the lead shield falls away to reveal an intricate crystalline structure inside. You recognize it immediately as an alien life form. It communicates with you telepathically in a strange code—which you somehow understand. The alien life form explains its predicament.

Turn to page 55.

62

"I would love to visit your world," you say, "but I have too many things to finish on this one right now."

"Very well," the alien emissary responds. "I will leave this crystal pendant with you. It is a hyperspace communicator. When you are ready to visit us, you need only activate its core with your mind, and a spaceship will be sent to you. Now, before I go, I must repay the 'hospitality' of the creatures that tricked me into coming here."

You hear a chorus of anguished animal cries throughout the house. Then silence. Your mind scan tells you that the chimpanzees have been thrown into a hyperspace prison. There they will float in a nameless void until they have served out their sentence.

The spaceship vanishes. When you return to your body, you find the crystal pendant hanging around your neck. The prison itself has vanished, along with the house that stood over it, and you and the professor find yourselves standing in the center of a broad, empty lawn.

The End

You decide you'd better call the police. This could be too much to handle alone.

You pick up the radio-telephone in your car, dial your friend Sergeant Morrison, and explain briefly what has happened.

"I get a lot of complaints about that place," says the sergeant. "People talk about bright, flashing lights before dawn, loud electronic noises, and weird-looking trucks going in and out at night. Not to mention the chimpanzees acting as guard dogs. We'd always assumed it was the neighbors' imaginations. If what you're telling me is true, we could have a dangerous situation on our hands."

"Do you want me to investigate more?" you ask.

"No, stay there," he says. "I'll be over in the squad car right away. Don't do anything. Just wait a couple of blocks from the house until I get there."

A squad car? Like all detectives, you know that it's almost impossible to catch criminals in the act after the cops have arrived.

If you follow his instructions and wait in the car, turn to the next page.

If you can't resist the temptation to go back for another look, turn to page 77.

While you wait, you try Ricardo and Lisa again. Yes! They're home. You explain the situation and you give your location, and soon they arrive on their bicycles. The three of you sit in your car discussing the case.

"Hey," says Lisa, "just suppose that Marsden is a ghost in human form."

"Can't be," replies Ricardo. "Ghosts don't take solid, human form. Sure, you can see a ghost's image, but they don't have real bodies. I don't think so, anyway."

"We still don't know whether Henry Marsden is a ghost or a real person," you remind them. "So let's not jump to any conclusions before we have a few more facts."

"I'd like to go up the road and get a look at this house," says Ricardo.

"Sergeant Morrison said to wait here until he gets here," you say. "He's going to be mad if we don't."

The car phone rings. It is the police operator calling to say that Sergeant Morrison will be delayed on an emergency call.

"That does it," says Lisa. "I think we should leave a note on the car for him and then do a little investigating on our own."

If you are firm about waiting for the sergeant, go on to the next page.

If you let Ricardo and Lisa talk you into going up to the house, turn to page 79.

"We have to wait for the sergeant," you say. "But I think we can get a glimpse of the house from a little way up the road, and still see the squad car when he arrives."

"I saw a restaurant about a half-mile back down the road," says Ricardo. "I'm going to bike down there and pick up some cheeseburgers, fries, and milkshakes for all of us. Might as well make a picnic dinner of it while we keep an eye on things. I bet nothing's going to happen anyway."

Ricardo is back in fifteen minutes with the food. You find a spot under a tree not far from the fence that borders the land around the house. You are close enough to catch a glimpse of the house through the trees, but not close enough to be noticed by anyone inside.

It is already late afternoon. The summer sun slants through the trees, but it is still hot out. The air itself is still and stifling, without a hint of a breeze. You sit back against a tree, a burger in one hand and a shake in the other. Mmmm! They're delicious. Why does drinking the shake make you feel so sleepy? In a minute you feel yourself falling asleep.

Suddenly you wake up. It is pitch-black all around you. What is this? Your hands and feet are bound with cord. Where are Ricardo and Lisa?

Turn to page 67.

You are still groggy with the kind of grogginess that you had from the anesthesia when you had your tooth pulled. You smell a strange aroma. It could be rotting flowers. Roses? Marigolds?

Furthermore, you are not alone. There is someone or something breathing—almost whimpering—near you. You struggle for a moment with the cords on your wrists and ankles. Then you remember your ring with the small, but very sharp, concealed blade. You scrape the ring against the hard surface under you to release the spring mechanism of the blade. Fortunately, the ring is positioned so that you can just cut the cord without cutting your wrist.

With your hands free, you quickly cut the cord binding your feet. You rub your arms and legs to restore circulation. They are still numb, but feeling is coming back—all pins and needles for a while. When your eyes grow adjusted to the darkness, you see that you are in a room with stone walls and a concrete floor. In the far corner stands a white-haired man, bent with age.

Turn to the next page.

68

Carefully you rise and advance toward him. He stands mute and still, as if paralyzed. He doesn't seem to know that you are there.

"Hello?" you say. There is no response.

Then you notice the chains fastened to his feet. You bend down and examine the shackles to see if there is any way to get them off, but they are old and rusty with rather primitive locks. You straighten up, but the man still doesn't seem to notice you. He seems to be in a trance.

If you try to wake him, he may help you figure out where you are and what is going on. But what are you going to do about his chains? It might be faster to leave him alone and come back later with help.

If you decide to stay with the old man and try to help him, turn to page 72.

If you think it would be best to go in search of help, turn to page 97.

You turn your mental powers against the door of the cell. You stand straight but not rigid, and focus your psychic energy on the locking mechanism. You feel the energy flowing from you. Harder now. Concentrate! Your mind traces the intricate locking sequence. There! It's open.

You and the professor start down the corridor toward the garage when *ZAP!* The two of you are frozen in mid-step by a force far greater than the chimpanzees possess. In their tinkering with the physical and psychic world, the chimpanzees have unleashed an evil force—a force powerful beyond human understanding.

As the force intensifies, you fight back with the vast power of your own mind. The corridor begins to glow with a soft orange color. Flashes of artificial lightning play along the walls. Your energy begins to drain. The violence of the conflict between you and this evil force is so great that it begins to destroy the fabric of time and space itself. Slowly you and the professor fade until you disappear into another dimension of the universe.

The End

"My name is Marsden, Professor Marsden. I was using the chimpanzees in my experiments to create superhumans. Instead I created superchimps."

"How did you—?" you begin to ask.

"I developed a super-energizing chamber that will give anyone advanced mental powers. And I think I have an idea for how it can help us get out of here.

"The cell we're in right now is part of an old prison complex built just after the Civil War. The prisoners in the old prison had been trying to dig a tunnel to freedom from this very cell, but they only succeeded in digging to another part of the prison. The tunnel leads directly to my laboratory!"

"Okay, Professor, let's go," you say.

You go first, crawling on your hands and knees and feeling your way along the tunnel. Soon you come to the inside of a loosely constructed stone wall. You can see into the brightly lit laboratory through the small cracks in the wall.

"I only see one chimp in there," you whisper. "If I can get in there, I can get him with my knockout-gas gun."

"One good push," the professor whispers back, "and this part of the wall will fall outward."

Turn to page 58.

72

You take your penknife out of your pocket. Maybe the blade is small enough...Yes! You're able to slide it into the mechanism. You feel the tumbler turn. In no time at all, you have the shackles off the man's feet. Then you shake him gently by the shoulders. He pulls away and cowers against the wall.

"Don't hit me! Don't hit me!" he moans.

"I'm not going to hurt you," you say.

The old man looks up with a startled expression. "Who...who are you?" he asks.

"I got a phone call from somebody named Marsden, and I traced the call to this house," you answer.

"Thank God, then," he says, "my call got through. I read about you in the papers. I knew you would help me." The old man extends a shaky hand.

"I am Henry Marsden. I live next to the ruins of my great-grandfather's prison. Part of the ruins extend under the house—that is where we are now. I have always been a recluse. A cruel gang of counterfeiters found out about it. They broke into my house and took it over as their headquarters."

"Can you walk?"

"I don't know," he says. "You'd better go on without me. I'll just slow you down."

---

*If you think you might find out more
if you explore the old prison complex
first, go on to the next page.*

*If you decide that you must escape immediately
with the old man, turn to page 75.*

"You'd better stay here until I can take a careful look around," you say. "I want to find out what we're up against."

"Be careful," says the old man. "The counterfeiters will stop at nothing."

"I'll be careful." You start out the door. You find yourself in a long, wide corridor with empty cells on either side.

Suddenly excited shouts and gunshots come from somewhere near the other end of the corridor. There is silence for a few moments. Then you are caught in the beam of a powerful electric light.

Turn to the next page.

"Thank goodness you're there," someone says. It is the voice of Sergeant Morrison. He shouts back behind him, "Lisa, Ricardo, come quick! I've found our missing detective."

Ricardo and Lisa come running toward you. You greet each other happily. Ricardo and Lisa, you find out, had been tied up in another part of the underground complex. The police had found them first when they raided the place and arrested the gang.

"You deserve a lot of credit," says Sergeant Morrison, "for alerting us to this place. We have the gang on charges of counterfeiting, homicide—we found the body of that man you told us about down here—kidnapping, and keeping chimpanzees within the city limits without a license."

The End

"Let's get out of here. Come on, follow me," you say to the old man.

"I can't move too fast," he protests. "It might be better if you leave me here and go for help."

"If I leave you here," you say, "the counterfeiters might come back and kill you before I can return. This door seems to be unlocked, but it's stuck. Let's see if we can get it open."

You push as hard as you can, but the door moves only a fraction of an inch.

"Here, let me try that," says the old man. He pushes the door lightly, and it goes flying off its hinges and down the hallway.

"You're really strong for an old man," you say.

"Nothing to it," says the old man. "I've got some life in me yet."

You are really amazed at how strong the old man has suddenly become, but you don't have time to think about it at the moment. The most important thing now is to get out of this dungeon.

Turn to page 81.

You're too tense to wait for Sergeant Morrison. You leave a note on your windshield for him and go back to the fence around the house. You creep along the outside of the fence. After a few hundred feet, the fence leads into dense woods. Not far into the woods, you come to another gate—a small one—in the fence. An overgrown road leads to the estate through this gate. You are trying to decide if you should follow the road in when a man with a broad scar across his face steps from behind a tree. He's wearing an old-fashioned prison uniform, but the laser pistol he has in his hand certainly looks modern enough.

"Okay, now turn around and go through that gate, and around to the back of the house," orders the man, "and no funny business. I'm behind you all the way with this gun."

You have no choice but to do as he says. Even your karate training will not help you here. He has you covered.

Turn to the next page.

As the two of you approach the house, the back door opens automatically. Inside there is a long corridor. As you walk down it, your footsteps are muted by the thick green carpeting on the floor. The corridor seems endless, but finally you come to a large steel door. You and the man behind you stop.

The man places his right hand on a small light blue screen next to the door. A beam of laser light passes up and down the screen, scanning his handprint.

There is a click. Then a hard metallic voice comes from a speaker over the door. "Identify yourselves. State purpose of visit. Remain standing exactly where you are. Repeat, do not move. Remain where you are."

"Security Agent 31X reporting with intruder."

There is silence for a moment, with only the sound of the air conditioning and exhaust fans buzzing in your ears. Then the door swings open, and the man behind you pushes you roughly into the room.

Turn to page 80.

The three of you walk up the road to a spot along the fence where you have a clear view of the house.

"I think we should get as close as possible," says Lisa.

"Look over there," says Ricardo. "There are lots of bushes on the other side of the house. I think we could get right up close without being seen."

"You're forgetting those crazy chimpanzees I told you about," you say.

As you try to decide what to do, you hear a faint scream from the direction of the house.

"Did you hear that?" asks Lisa. "Now we have to investigate."

"All right," you say, "but let's be very careful."

The three of you run along the fence, which is broken in places, until you find a break in it large enough to squeeze through. Being careful to keep the shrubbery between you and the house, the three of you sneak up to the basement windows. You try to peer inside, but the windows are all silvered from the inside, like mirrors. All you see are your own faces.

Then, before you know it, all three of you are surrounded by five snarling chimpanzees. They're huge, and their teeth look very sharp.

Turn to page 84.

80

A group of men and women sit at an oval table. In front of each person is a glass of water, a pad of paper, and a pen. They are well-dressed and all seem to be about fifty to sixty years old. The scene looks for all the world like a typical business meeting of any large corporation. They all turn to look as you enter. They look serious, but not really hostile.

A white-haired man in a dark blue pinstripe suit smiles briefly and asks, "Well, now that you are here, what can we do for you?"

"I was investigating a telephone call asking for my help. The call came from this address."

The man speaks again. "The telephone call was unfortunate. It came from someone who has recently been released from a foreign prison. He was a brave man—a scientist and a leader for freedom in his country. He was in a bad mental state. We regret that our care did not keep him alive. His fears were too much for him. Do you understand?"

"Perhaps," you say, "but I need more of an explanation than that. This whole setup looks peculiar to me."

"Very well," says the man, "I will explain."

Turn to page 82.

The door leads to a hallway filled with dazzling white light. You enter the hallway with the old man following you. You turn to look at him for a second. He seems to be getting younger by the minute. His hair is now dark. He looks a lot like your father. Wait! It is your father. He is saying "Wake up... wake up...."

You're still in the woods outside the house. Ricardo and Lisa are there too. And so is Sergeant Morrison.

"I wasn't captured?" you ask. "Wasn't the milkshake drugged?"

"I think you were just feeling the effects of the warm weather," says your father.

"It was probably best you were asleep," adds Sergeant Morrison. "We raided the house and arrested the whole gang. Even recovered a dead body as they were trying to bury it in the basement. Your father came right over when I called him a short time ago. He was worried about you."

"Don't feel bad about not being in on the action at the end," says your father. "You did your part and the police did theirs. That's the way it should be. We are still mighty proud of you."

The End

"We are the International Planning Group, a private organization made up of representatives from different parts of the world. We are dedicated to energy conservation and the peaceful development of natural resources everywhere."

"But why hide out here in this little town?" you ask.

"This is only one of our meeting groups. We have many other places such as this, as well as various research facilities throughout the world. In this location we use the name of Marsden as cover. Our security agents in prison dress, and their trained chimpanzees, scare off most intruders. We would be honored if you would join our organization. We try to recruit the best minds in each of our operational areas, and we need younger minds with fresh viewpoints."

All the faces in the room are looking at you and smiling.

"You don't have to make up your mind right now," says the man. "Take your time, and contact us when you have made a decision. Any young friends of yours that you could recommend will also be welcome in our organization."

As you walk back to your car to meet Sergeant Morrison, you still don't know what to believe, but you have a lot to think about.

The End

84

As the chimpanzees get closer, it becomes clear that they are trying to back you up against the basement door. You have no choice but to open the door and go in. It is pitch-black inside. You feel along the side of the door and find a light switch. You flip it.

The three of you are in a large, modern office with mahogany paneling and steel and glass desks. In the center of the room is a large conference table. On it, spread from one end to the other, is a collection of blueprints. You go over and take a look. One of the papers is labeled:

TOP SECRET INVASION PLANS
EARTH-WESTERN HEMISPHERE-
PHASE ALPHA

You rifle through more of the papers. They are filled with dates, graphs, and calculations of various sorts—figures for agricultural output, natural resources, and energy production of various power plants.

As you look through the papers, a tall, very thin man-like creature with an oversized head enters the office at the far end. What is he? You've never seen anyone—or thing—like him.

Go on to the next page.

"Ah, my inquisitive friends, I see you are examining our plans," he says. "Go ahead, be my guests. Look all you want. It does not matter. Our plans are already in motion."

"Are you—" you stammer. "Are you...an alien?" You've read about them but never been sure they were out there.

The alien seems to look at the three of you with both intensity and amusement.

"I make a proposal," he says. "Why not join us? We could use Earthlings like you to help us. Earlier today, we tried to recruit another Earthling, but he ran out on us. However, I think you three will be more sensible."

There's no way you will seriously take him up on his offer. But by going along with him, you might find a way to stop the aliens' plan. On the other hand, it might be better just to stand and fight.

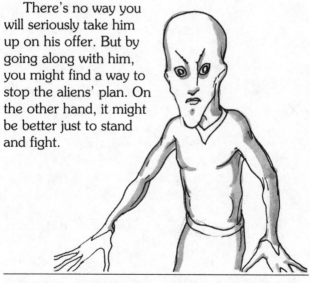

If you pretend to join, turn to the next page.

If you refuse, turn to page 88.

86

You figure the best thing to do is to humor this creature. And you have to admit, you are curious. Where did he come from?

"Come now, my friends," says the man. "It's not all that bad. We will train you for your new positions. We guarantee job security, and even a pension after a certain number of years. Perhaps one of you would like to be an Earth project manager, or perhaps an Invasion Commander like myself."

Turn to page 94.

The three of you jump into your car and drive down to the Hedge Brook police station. Your old friend Sergeant Morrison is glad to see you and meet your friends. You tell the sergeant about the phone call and about the information in the history book.

"I think you should tell all this to Detective Murphy," he says. "There is definitely more to the old Marsden place than meets the eye."

Detective Murphy turns out to be a pipe smoking middle-aged man in a tweed jacket. He looks more like a college professor than a detective.

"I already have a file on the Marsden place," says Detective Murphy. "That house has been deserted for years. I've come to the conclusion that it is haunted. Now I know that sounds unscientific and unprofessional, but it's the only idea I've been able to come up with in light of the evidence. The house is notorious in that neighborhood—strange lights at night, and strange noises at every time of day."

"You mean you believe in ghosts?" asks Lisa.

"I'm sure your amateur detective friend here will confirm that we detectives do not believe in anything. We let the facts speak for themselves."

"What is that supposed to mean?" asks Lisa.

"It means precisely what I mean it to mean," says Murphy, "and furthermore, if you like, I'll turn the Marsden case over to the three of you."

Turn to page 90.

"No, thanks," you say. "We're not interested."

"You refuse, do you?" shouts the creature. "Well, we have another use for humans. In fact, it is our main use for humans."

With that, he takes out a small device from his pocket and aims it at the three of you. A beam of incredibly cold light—its temperature hundreds of degrees below zero—freezes you, Lisa, and Ricardo into solid blocks of ice.

Then the man takes out a rubber stamp from his other pocket and stamps your forehead:

HUMAN MEAT—GALACTIC PRIME
SOURCE—PLANET EARTH
GRADE A

The End

Detective Murphy sits back in his chair and takes a few puffs on his pipe. For a moment, he looks deep in thought.

"What I want you three to do is to keep a watch on that place—from a safe distance, and only during the day. Is that understood?" he says.

The three of you leave the police station. You're hooked. This is your kind of adventure.

First you go back to your house to pick up your two-way radio-communicator. Each is small enough to be hidden inside a pocket, and they have a range of over seven miles.

Then you drive over to the Marsden house. As you drive by slowly, you see that it is a large, modern house set back from the main road.

"I thought only old houses could look spooky," you say.

You park the car across the road and sit watching the house for an hour or so. All the windows of the house are closed, and all of the curtains are drawn. The front door looks partly open, though.

"It certainly is stuffy in the car," says Lisa.

"More like boring, I'd say," says Ricardo.

"What do you say we go over and take a closer look?" says Lisa. "Ghosts only come out at night anyway—if there are such things."

"Detective Murphy told us not to, but I think we should," you say.

Turn to the next page.

The three of you reach the front door. It is slightly ajar and opens with a light touch. You peer inside. No furniture. Nothing. No sign of life.

"I'll go and investigate," you say. "Let's keep in touch with the two-way radios. I have one of them here in my shirt pocket, and the other is in the car. When I know that it's safe, I'll radio for you two to come in. I don't know why, but something tells me this place is dangerous."

You step inside.

WHAM! The front door slams shut behind you. You try the doorknob. No good! It won't budge. Then you notice that there are no windows in the foyer, which leads into a hallway, also without windows. Yet there is a strange half-light coming from somewhere. The air is stiflingly hot. It seems to grow hotter by the minute. You try your radio, but only get static.

If you concentrate on trying to get the front door open, go on to the next page.

If you decide to search the rest of the house, turn to page 99.

You push against the door. No good. You take out your penknife and probe inside the keyhole to feel out the mechanism. A little leverage, and the tumbler turns. You try the doorknob, and the door pulls open.

But what is this?

The door doesn't open to the outside any more. In front of you is a wide stone stairway leading down into the ground. Something beyond your control seems to compel you to go down. At the bottom of the stairway, you find yourself in a large underground room. In the half-gloom, you make out what look like thick stone walls. At the far end of the room is a row of dark prison cells. In one of the cells you see a faint phosphorescent glow several feet from the floor. The glow emits a low hum. Mesmerized, you walk toward it. The hum becomes louder and begins to change into an eerie buzzing voice.

"ZZZZzzzzz . . . . .myzzz. . . . . . . .nameizzzz . . . . .Henry Marzzz. . . . . . . .den."

The voice becomes more distinct.

"I need your help...help..."

The glow begins to expand. A ghostly form starts to materialize.

Turn to page 102.

94

As he is talking, the man walks over and opens the outside door. He beckons to you to go out. As you step out, you realize that you are in big trouble. The sky is almost covered by an enormous space vehicle. It is bright gold in color and it hovers overhead with a low humming sound.

You wonder if you will enjoy your new life.

The End

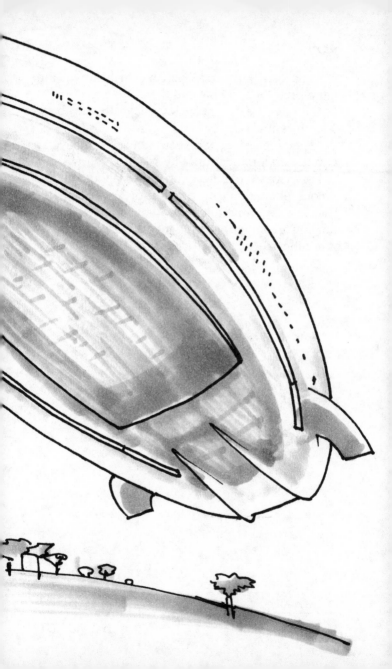

96

"You can be anyone, anyone in history," the figure says. "All you have to do is choose."

"I'll give it a try," you say. "Can I come back when I want to, like before?"

"That depends on who you choose. You have to wish it, and that might not be so easy."

For several minutes you think about all the famous people you have heard of or read about. Then a wild impulse leaps to your mind—so wild that you are embarrassed to mention it. You'll think of another...

Turn to page 101.

You feel that it is important to help the old man, but you must also find out if Ricardo and Lisa are all right. The last thing you remember is that the three of you were having a picnic under a tree. If you can get out of this place and contact Sergeant Morrison, you can come back and rescue the old man.

On one side of the dungeon room is a large closed door made of rough wood and bolted with wide iron bars. Cautiously you try the heavy metal latch. The door moves. It's unlocked. Whoever tied you up probably never thought you would be able to get loose. You push open the door very slowly, hoping it won't creak. You peer out into the dark gloom of the corridor. It is empty and silent. Quickly and silently you head for the door at the end of the corridor. Halfway there it happens.

WHAM!

Turn to page 33.

You run down the dimly lit hallway and come to a large windowless room. Darn! Why doesn't this place have any windows? You saw enough of them from the outside. There is a deep alcove set in the wall on one side of the room. A light in the alcove flicks on, revealing the figure of a man. You can see only his head and face, which are horribly burned. The rest of the figure is shrouded in a dark cape.

"I am the ghost of Henry Marsden. Here on this site, where my evil actions cost so many their lives, I have been given a machine by the spirits—a machine that defies time: past, present, and future. To atone for my sins, I must forever act as a teacher, to lead whoever comes here to greater wisdom and humility than my own. Turn and look behind you."

Turn to the next page.

100

You do as he says and two figures materialize—one is a baby, the other is an old man. You can't tell if they are real people, or images made of light. Every few seconds they flicker and twist.

"Hey, that's my watch," you say, stepping closer to the old man. Suddenly you understand. "Hey," you say, "Is that—?"

"They're both you," says the ghost. "You as a baby, and as an old man."

"Why are they here?"

"It is a test. Choose one."

You are dying with curiosity. Being a baby—that's something you'll never be able to remember on your own. But as an old man, you'd know everything that was going to happen to you in your life.

If you choose to be a baby, turn to page 104.

If you choose old age, turn to page 105.

But once the wish is formed, the process begins. No! You want to take it back. You don't really want to be Genghis Khan.

The End

"I need your help. My spirit is condemned to haunt this godforsaken prison until my soul is released. You can help me."

"Who, me?" you ask.

"Yes. I beg you to release my soul. I ask forgiveness. If you only say you forgive me, I will be released. Say it. Please say it."

"Now hold on a moment," you say. "First I need some facts to go on before I forgive anyone. I read the history book account. It says you were the warden of this place."

"That's right, I was."

"And the conditions were terrible in the prison," you say.

"But I had no money to help. I only had funds enough to give the prisoners turnip soup, and a few potatoes now and then. I ate no better, I swear it."

"Then why is your soul condemned to suffer, if it wasn't your fault?"

"It was the fire, you see. I set it. But I did not intend to kill anybody. I only wanted to destroy the prison. The prisoners were always ready to riot. I lived in constant fear of them. I thought they would all escape the fire. I did not know any of them would be trapped inside. I died in the fire myself."

"Then why is your soul...?"

"I still blame myself. I cannot forgive myself for my stupidity—even if my intentions were good. Only a human soul can forgive me."

"All right, then, you are forgiven."

Turn to page 106.

104

A baby again. For some period of time—it could be minutes, it could be years, babies don't understand time—you just enjoy the sensation of amplified sound and wonder. You see the world through new eyes. You cannot understand what the giant people are saying. You try to stand. Oops! You fall down. The floor is so hard. How helpless you feel. You struggle with your first words.

You are filled with a sense of energy. You can do anything! You use that energy to remember that you are not a baby…And somewhere in your mind you remember. You are not a baby. "I'm a detective —I've got to get back," you say to yourself.

ZAP! You reenter your own age. It feels like an electric shock. You are a bit stiff after the experience. You look up. The figure in the cape is staring at you again.

"You did that well," he says. "Now you can leave. Or, if you are feeling adventurous, how would you like the experience of being another person?"

If you accept, turn to page 96.

If you decline, turn to page 108.

Why did you choose old age? Curiosity, you guess. At least you know you'll live a long, long time. You see that you have cracked and very wrinkled hands. Your body trembles slightly. Your eyesight seems good, but you can't hear very well. You search your mind for memories of the years since you were a teenager. Funny, you can't seem to remember anything. They have all faded away.

You are so tired. You will just sleep for a while. Thinking takes so much energy.

You drop off into a light sleep. Your heart slows, skips a beat or so, then stops. It is all over.

The End

106

There is a blinding flash of light. You shade your eyes from it.

You hear, "Thank you, thank yoooo…"

The image of Marsden is gone. You run up the stone stairway and through the door at the top. But as you do, you find yourself running outside— smack into Ricardo, Lisa, and Detective Murphy. You almost knock them down.

"I thought I told you just to watch the house from a safe distance," says Detective Murphy, very sternly, "but anyway, I'm glad you're all right. You are all right, aren't you?"

"I sure am," you say, "and I don't think we'll be seeing any weird lights from this place from now on."

The End

108

You remember that Ricardo and Lisa are waiting outside. You call them on your radio.

"Hello, Ricardo... Lisa... are you there?"

"We hear you. Everything all right in there?"

"I'm all right, I guess. Kind of hard to explain. I'm getting some kind of lessons from the ghost of Henry Marsden. I'll be out soon, I hope."

Then static.

The ghostly figure gestures toward you again.

"I said you could leave, but I didn't say with whom."

As he says this, Marsden's head grows larger and larger, until it turns into an enormous disc shaped object. It begins to glow with a unique brightness. Then the room disappears, and the disc expands to huge size. Portholes appear around its middle. A hatch swings open. Music comes from inside—electronic music. You enter this machine, and in a millisecond you are whisked away to other galaxies.

You don't know if you are going to like this lesson or not.

The End

ABOUT THE ARTIST

Illustrator: Sittisan Sundaravej (Quan).
Sittisan is a resident of Bangkok, Thailand and an old fan of *Choose Your Own Adventure*. He attended The University of the Arts in Philadelphia, where he received his BSC in architecture and a BFA for animation. He has been a 2D and 3D animation director for productions in Asia and the United States and is a freelance illustrator.

ABOUT THE AUTHOR

R. A. Montgomery attended Hopkins Grammar School, Williston-Northhampton School and Williams College where he graduated in 1958. Montgomery was an adventurer all his life, climbing mountains in the Himalaya, skiing throughout Europe and scuba-diving wherever he could. His interests included education, macro-economics, geo-politics, mythology, history, mystery novels and music. He wrote his first interactive book, *Journey Under the Sea*, in 1976 and published it under the series name *The Adventures of You*. A few years later Bantam Books bought this book and gave Montgomery a contract for five more, to inaugurate their new children's publishing division. Bantam renamed the series *Choose Your Own Adventure* and a publishing phenomenon was born. The series has sold more than 260 million copies in over 40 languages.

For games, activities, and other fun stuff, or to write to Chooseco, visit us online at cyoa.com

The History of "Gamebooks"

Although the Choose Your Own Adventure series, first published in 1976, may be the best known example of interactive fiction, it was not the first.

In 1941, the legendary South American writer Jorge Luis Borges published *Examen de la obra de Herbert Quain*, a short story that contained three parts and nine endings. He followed that with his better known work, *El Jardin de Senderos que se bifurcan,* or *The Garden of Forking Paths*, a novel about a writer lost in a garden maze that had multiple story lines and endings.

Jorge Luis Borges

More than 20 years later, in 1964, another famous South American writer, Julio Cortazar, published a novel called *Rayuela* or *Hopscotch*. This book was composed of 155 "chapters" and the reader could make their way through a number of different "novels" depending on choices they made. At the same time, French author

Julio Cortazar

Raymond Queneau wrote an interactive story entitled *Un conte à votre façon*, or *A Story As You Like It*.

Early in the 1970s, a popular series for children called *Trackers* was published in the UK that contained multiple choices and endings. In 1976,

Journey Under the Sea,
1st Edition

R. A. Montgomery wrote and published the first interactive book for young adults: *Journey Under the Sea* under the series name *The Adventures of You.* This was changed to *Choose Your Own Adventure* by Bantam Books when they published this and five others to launch the series in 1979. The success of CYOA spawned many imitators and the term "gamebooks" came into use to refer to any books that utilized the second person "you" to tell a story using multiple choices and endings.

Montgomery said in an interview in 2013: "This wasn't traditional literature. *The New York Times* children's book reviewer called Choose Your Own Adventure a literary movement. Indeed it was. The most important thing for me has always been to get kids reading. It's not the format, it's not even the writing. The reading happened because kids were in the driver's seat. They were the mountain climber, they were the doctor, they were the deep-sea explorer. They made choices, and so they read. There were people who expressed the feeling that nonlinear literature wasn't 'normal.' But interactive books have a long history, going back 70 years."

Young R. A. Montgomery

Choose Your Own Adventure Timeline

1977 – R.A. Montgomery writes *Journey Under the Sea* under the pen name Robert Mountain. It is published by Vermont Crossroads Press along with the title *Sugar Cane Island* under the series name "Adventures of You."

1979 – Montgomery brings his book series to New York where it is rejected by 14 publishers before being purchased by Bantam Books for the brand new children's division. The new series is re-named *Choose Your Own Adventure*.

1980 – *Space and Beyond* initial sales are slow until Bantam seeds libraries across the U.S. with 100,000 free copies.

1983 – CYOA sales reach ten million units of the first 14 titles.

1984 – For a six week period, 9 spots of the top 15 books on the Waldenbooks Children's Bestseller's list belong to CYOA. *Choose* dominates the list throughout the 1980s.

1989 – Ten years after its original publication, over 150 *Choose Your Own* titles have been published.

1990 – R. A. Montgomery publishes the TRIO series with Bantam, a six-book series that draws inspiration from future worlds in CYOA titles *Escape* and *Beyond Escape*.

1992 – ABC TV adapts Shannon Gilligan's CYOA title *The Case of the Silk King* as a made-for-TV movie. It is set in Thailand and stars Pat Morita, Soleil Moon Frye and Chad Allen.

1995 – A horror trend emerges in the children's book market, and Bantam launches *Choose Your Own Nightmare*, a series of shorter CYOA titles focused on creepy themes. The subseries is translated into several languages and converted to DVD and computer games.

1998 – Bantam licenses property from *Star Wars* to release *Choose Your Own Star Wars Adventures*. The 3-book series features traditional CYOA elements to place the reader in each of the existing *Star Wars* films and feature holograms on the covers.

2003 – With the series virtually out of print, the copyright licenses and the *Choose Your Own Adventure* trademark revert to R. A. Montgomery. He forms Chooseco LLC with Shannon Gilligan.

2005 – *Choose Your Own Adventure* is re-launched into the education market, with all new art and covers. Texts have been updated to reflect changes to technology and discoveries in archeology and science.

2006 – Chooseco LLC, operating out of a renovated farmhouse in Waitsfield, Vermont, publishes the series for the North American retail market, shipping 900,000 copies in its first six months.

2008 – Chooseco publishes CYOA *The Golden Path*, a three volume epic for readers 10+, written by Anson Montgomery.

2008 – Poptropica and Chooseco partner to develop the first branded Poptropica island, "Nabooti Island" based on CYOA #4, *The Lost Jewels of Nabooti*.

2009 – *Choose Your Own Adventure* celebrates 30 years in print and releases two titles in partnership with WADA, the World Anti-Doping Agency, to emphasize fairness in sport.

2010 – Chooseco launches a new look for the classic books using special neon ink.

2011 – Reads of *Fabulous Terrible*, Chooseco's YA novel for girls, reach 1 million on Wattpad.com

2013 – Chooseco launches eBooks on Kindle and in the iBookstore with trackable maps and other bonus features. The project is briefly hung up when Apple has to rewrite its terms and conditions for publishers to create space for this innovative eBook type.

2014 – Brazil and Korea license publishing rights to the series. 20 foreign publishers currently distribute the series worldwide.

2014 – Beloved series founder R.A. Montgomery dies at age 78. He finishes his final book in the Choose Your Own Adventure series only weeks before.

2015 – Anson Montgomery's "lost title" original #185 *Escape from the Haunted Warehouse* receives glowing reviews from *People Magazine* and CBC Radio, and he is included with 24 other writers in the 2015 Twitter Fiction Festival.

Danger Trivia Quiz

How many adventures did you take through the House of Danger? If you can't solve this trivia quiz, perhaps you should take a few more.

1) What is the name that appears on your phone tracer after the mysterious call?
A. Harold Marshen
B. Henry Marsden
C. Harry Master
D. George Washington

2) What type of animal appears in front of the house you are investigating, frightening you?
A. Hippos
B. Gorillas
C. Bunny Rabbits
D. Chimpanzees

3) What is unique about the paper you take from the dying man?
A. It has red and blue flecks in it, like currency paper.
B. It has a message in secret code written on it.
C. It is torn into the shape of a chimpanzee.
D. It has a map of the old prison on it.

4) What is located on the site of the old prison now?
A. An amusement park.
B. A new prison.
C. A large glass house.
D. A pig farm.

5) What kind of plants does the strange woman with the high voice keep in the house?
A. Marigolds and Daisies.
B. An orange tree.
C. A rose bush.
D. Venus fly traps.

6) What is surprising about the man in the back seat who holds a gun to your head?
A. He is actually a talking chimpanzee.
B. He is actually Henry Marsden.
C. There isn't actually anyone in the back seat.
D. He has a funny looking nose.

7) Where did the chimpanzees get their knowledge of technology?
A. From Henry Marsden.
B. From the ruins of the prison.
C. Chimpanzees are just naturally smart, they knew all about it for ages.
D. From an alien that they had tricked into coming to Earth.

8) What were the people in the Marsden house doing?
A. Counterfeiting money and keeping chimpanzees without a permit.
B. Baking cookies and pies.
C. Planning to rob a bank.
D. Hiding from the true owner of the house.

9) What did Professor Marsden create through his experiments?
A. A space travel machine.
B. A potion to travel through time.
C. Super chimps.
D. A new flavor of ice cream.

10) What does the special chamber you go into do?
A. Makes you invisible.
B. Gives you super strength.
C. Gives you a quiet place to collect your thoughts.
D. Gives you intense mental and psychic powers.

WORLD'S GREATEST UNSOLVED MYSTERIES

THE TAOS HUM

Throughout the small town of Taos, New Mexico, a buzz can be heard that sounds like a distant diesel engine. While humans hear it, sound recording devices often do not. The source of the sound remains unknown.

A triangle over the ocean with points at Miami, Bermuda and Puerto Rico has sucked in at least 16 air and seacraft. Pilots describe jumbled controls and equipment failure. The U.S. Navy does not consider the Triangle a legitimate threat, and no official maps note it—yet the staggering number of lost craft suggest a mystery is afoot.

THE BERMUDA TRIANGLE

JACK THE RIPPER

A serial killer who haunted England in the 1800s was never located, and continues to haunt local legends.

Sightings of an enormous lake monster shaped like a dinosaur began in 1933 and continue to this day. Yet no one has solid proof that the creature of Loch Ness, in the Scottish Highlands, definitely exists.

THE LOCH NESS MONSTER

BIGFOOT

In Nepal, the yeti; in the Pacific Northwest, the Sasquatch: a big hairy humanoid who walks upright. So many have seen one tromping through the forest but no one can prove it. More than one scientist has devoted a career to locating evidence of their existence.

These prehistoric (3,000 - 2,000 B.C.) rocks in Wiltshire, England definitely exist, but no one is certain of their exact purpose, or how they came to stand in a circle.

STONEHENGE

THE GREEN CHILDREN

In 12th century England, two children showed up in a small village called Woolpit with green skin, speaking an unknown language. They integrated into the village and learned English, but their history still remained a mystery: they said they followed a river of light leading to the town. Some believed they had come from the fabled Hollow Earth.

VITAL STATISTICS:
HOUSE OF DANGER

Deaths by Venus flytrap: 2

Encounters with Genghis Kahn: 1

Possible endings: 20

Alien abductions: 7

Slayings by chimpanzees: 4

AND 17 OTHERS AT CYOA.COM

CHOOSE YOUR OWN ADVENTURE® 1
THE ABOMINABLE SNOWMAN
CHOOSE FROM 28 ENDINGS!
BY R. A. MONTGOMERY

CHOOSE YOUR OWN ADVENTURE® 2

JOURNEY
UNDER THE SEA

CHOOSE
FROM 42
ENDINGS

BY R. A. MONTGOMERY

THE LOST JEWELS OF NABOOTI

CHOOSE
FROM 38
ENDINGS!

BY R. A. MONTGOMERY

MYSTERY OF THE MAYA

CHOOSE FROM 39 ENDINGS!

BY R. A. MONTGOMERY

HOUSE OF DANGER

CHOOSE FROM 20 ENDINGS!

BY R. A. MONTGOMERY

RACE FOREVER

CHOOSE FROM 33 ENDINGS!

BY R. A. MONTGOMERY

ESCAPE

CHOOSE FROM 27 ENDINGS

BY R. A. MONTGOMERY

LOST ON THE AMAZON

CHOOSE FROM 28 ENDINGS!

BY R. A. MONTGOMERY

TROUBLE ON PLANET EARTH

CHOOSE FROM 22 ENDINGS!

BY R. A. MONTGOMERY

SECRET
OF THE NINJA

BY JAY LEIBOLD

ISLAND OF TIME

CHOOSE FROM 12 ENDINGS!

BY R. A. MONTGOMERY

CHOOSE YOUR OWN ADVENTURE® 185
ESCAPE FROM THE HAUNTED WAREHOUSE
CHOOSE FROM 13 ENDINGS!
From the Lost Archives
BY ANSON MONTGOMERY